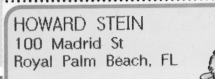
Do you know who does what job?

How many questions can you answer?
It's fun to peek behind
the flap — to see if you
were right...

PRICE/STERN/SLOAN
Publishers, Inc., Los Angeles

Who flies
an airplane?

Who delivers letters?

MAIL

Who works in a library?

Who fights fires?

Who works on board a fishing boat?

Who works in a garage?

Who looks after passengers on

Who looks for clues?

Who looks after sick animals?

Who works out in space?